DRUMS
of
SUNRISE

"….speak not my child, your father's corpse is still lying helpless. He has been defeated by his rivals. Why do you speak of coronation too soon or have you long awaited his death?"

Sixtus Chetachi Igbokwe

authorHOUSE®

AuthorHouse™
1663 Liberty Drive
Bloomington, IN 47403
www.authorhouse.com
Phone: 1 (800) 839-8640

Published by AuthorHouse 09/03/2015

ISBN: 978-1-5049-4865-4 (sc)
ISBN: 978-1-5049-4864-7 (e)

THIS BOOK IS DEDICATED TO
MY BELOVED PARENTS,

MR. JOSEPH IFEANYI IGBOKWE

AND

MRS. EUNICE ADAKU IGBOKWE.

My pride, my heroes,

Ndi Chukwu mere eze.

Ihe dika unu akokwala m.

FOREWORD

A Person can learn various arts and put them into practice.

Notwithstanding, the art of writing can be mastered but it cannot be practiced when and if the passion to write is not there. Sixtus Chetachi Igbokwe has in this novel *'Drums of Sunrise'* disclosed his intellectual identity, personality, capacity, potentiality and prowess in creative writing. The author used simple English in his narration.

I thank God that we are having people who are following the footsteps of Late Prof. Chinua Achebe, a winner of liquefied Natural Gas (L.N.G) for creative writers in the making. This book has a great message for our children and families, especially those who are still calling God's creatures outcasts. We are all one in unity with Jesus Christ.

It teaches love, hard work, dedication, perseverance, humility, patience and discourages pride, egotism, vainglory and deceit. I love to recommend that this book be made compulsory for all students. I also recommend it to the public. It is a must read for every home. I congratulate Sixtus Chetachi Igbokwe for the work well done.

DR. (MRS.) NMA OLEBARA (FCAI).

AUTHOR'S NOTE

The rising of the sun has been a very beautiful scenario for me from childhood. When I was younger, I would wake before the cockcrow and sit beside my grandmother's hut, to watch the sunrise.

It created a nice scene for me as I gazed into the sky wondering how possible it is for the sun to hang on the sky. My father had once told me that the sun did not make any special effort to hang on the sky perhaps the gods were in the best position to deliberate on its state.

The singing of the birds was another sight attraction for me as they flew across each palm tree in our small African compound. My mother, on her own path equally told me when I was younger that the early birds catch the worms but there is no food for the lazy ones.

I am an African and a true son of the soil. On the tips of my finger lies the entire scenario of life in an African-Igbo society. Yes, I'm saying that, as an African I am in the best position to tell the tale of an African society from sun rise to sunset.

I therefore enjoin you all to beat the 'Drums of Sunrise'.

SIXTUS CHETACHI IGBOKWE

Chapter 1

Today's sun is pale, and it is believed that the pale sun brings the rain. The women of Umuabali were already gathering their goods to be taken to the market, because it is an Eke Market day. Umuabali clan is the citadel of power among the various communities with which they share a common ancestry. Not only is that the capital clan, it also enjoys unchallenged primacy because no king comes out of the kingdom if not from Umuabali. Ani, the gods of the earth, and Amadioha, the gods of thunder, are believed to have made this rule more than twenty decades ago.

The role of Ani is far more than being a mere deity of the earth. In the Igbo belief, Ani is the custodian of customs and tradition, of fertility, and of public morality. Ani brings a lot of blessings to his worshipers and exposes an evildoer by bringing him to judgment. Igwekala, the gods of the skies, sanction Amadioha to strike anyone who commits an abomination. Victims of Amadioha punishment are not mourned because it is believed that Amadioha rightly punished them for atrocities to either their fellow human beings or to the gods.

The popular Ekeogu Market (which is in honor of Eke, the gods of benevolence) is situated at the center of Umuabali clan. The market operates only on Eke Market days, and it attracts hundreds of people, even those from the neighboring communities. The villagers have divided the market into two, leaving a bigger portion for the Diala to which most of them belong. A smaller portion was left for the Osu people, who are segregated because it is believed they were dedicated to the gods as slaves. They do not intermarry, and they are not conferred traditional titles. Anything contrary to this is regarded as abominable. Surrounded by these circumstances, most of the girls from Osu families remain unmarried and are stressed up till death.

Obianuju is a beautiful young girl from Umuabali clan. She was one of the few maidens who was remarkable for her hard work. She crowned this with her ability to dance well in the village square, which earned her a lot of admiration. Admiration for Obianuju also resulted from the circumstances surrounding her birth.

Nneoma, Obianuju's mother, was married for twenty years and childless. On the seventh week of that year's rainy season (which was preceded by the clearing of the bushes), Nneoma called upon Chukwu. As a result, she gave birth to Obianuju, and it was on that fateful morning that her grandmother, Adanma died. Her grandmother was a good woman, and it is believed that the gods do not terminate the life of the good. This led to the full conviction that Adanma must have been reincarnated in Obianuju.

To sum it all, the chief priest, Ezemmuo, said many good things about the child on the day of her birth, including, "From her, our land shall experience the true sunrise and the rains that will water our lives, and make us flourish like the palm tree."

Many people did not believe Ezemmuo's statements about the child because Obianuju came from an Osu family. They asked, "Can the gods bless an Osu?"

Obianuju came from a very poor family that found it difficult to provide their basic needs. Being a poor farmer, her father, Obiefuna, combined his farm work with palm wine tapping. He sent the wine to Nze Nduka, a prominent rich man in Umuaku, the place of his in-laws. Nze Nduka was very remarkable for the number of barns he owned. He was also a titled man and was given the title Ezeji for his remarkable success and outstanding farm work. (It is only those Ahiajoku has bestowed with fertility that are able to take up the Ezeji title.)

Obianuju helped her parents from her little savings. One Orie Market day, she paid for her mother's bill when her mother nearly died of snake bite. It was around noon on that fateful day when Nneoma was coming back from the market and was attacked by a snake. The village diviner who serves Agwu, the deity of divination, told Mazi Obiefuna to pay twenty cowries to cure the wife. Mazi Obiefuna was short of words. He stood beside his helpless wife and prayed to his Chi until Obianuju came and paid the bill from her little *esusu* savings.

Mazi Obiefuna, Obianuju's father, blessed her. He would often burst into tears when he remembered the fate Obianuju would soon face because of her status as an Osu.

The rain began to drizzle when Obianuju was in her small hut mending some of her torn clothes. She decided to go to the market to buy some food stuffs. It was becoming late and the sun was gradually setting. She hurriedly got to the market, bought the food stuff and started making her way back to the house. On her way, she met an old woman carrying a heavy basket of cassava, yam, and kola nut. Obianuju had pity on the old woman and decided to give her a helping hand, asking, "Mama, can I help you?"

The old woman was surprised. She couldn't believe there were still good youths who have kind hearts. While tightening her wrapper, she stared at Obianuju. "If you insist, my daughter."

Because she loved old people, Obianuju hurriedly carried the basket on her head amidst heavy rain. Old people reminded her of her grandmother, Adanma, whom she had been told was reincarnated in her. Tiny marks on the face of Adanma were also seen in that of Obianuju. The pointed nose and the dark hair were similar, but their Chi were not the same. Adanma's Chi led her into dying young after all her suffering, yet she was unable to ripen the fruits of her labors. She suffered from Agba, a sickness that was regarded as abominable because it was believed that Ezeani, the god of the earth, usually struck people who disobeyed him with that illness.

It never occurred to Obianuju that the old woman was Oriaku Eke, wife of Eke and the goddess of benevolence. It was believed that Eke usually sends out his wife to go to the market to inspect and buy kola nut for his visitors. The kola nut signifies life in Igbo tradition and culture.

When Obianuju and the old woman got to Nwafor River, the old woman refused to go further. She asked Obianuju to drop her basket, and Obianuju lowered the basket, breathing as one who had fought with a lion. "My daughter," the old woman said, "You have done well. You have shown me kindness in a small way, but I will show you benevolence in a bigger way." Obianuju became surprised and began to look at the old woman with keen interest. "My daughter," the old woman cleared her throat twice and continued. "You will get married, and your household will lead this kingdom. I am Oriaku Eke, the goddess of benevolence."

On hearing this, Obianuju started running away and screaming. She had heard of the story about Oriaku Eke but felt it was only a fairy tale. People who saw Obianuju running were afraid because they knew that Obianuju was not the kind of person to raise a false alarm.

On her arrival, Obianuju was panting heavily as if she had fought with a lion. She unfolded her experiences with the goddess of benevolence and the promises made to her. Mazi Ejemba, one of the elders of the land, was in doubt. He spoke against the goddess and made several offensive words against her. He even went further to curse the gods. When he was called to order, he continued to speak, and the gods became angry with him.

Chapter 2

Mazi Ejemba was in his *Obi,* cheering happily with friends, telling the story of the previous night and how a fearless lion went round the village, roaring at the top of its voice. Suddenly, he had an august visitor, the chief priest, Ezemmuo. The chief priest looked pale and troubled. On his right hand, he held a sack, signifying the anger of the gods. On the left was the *ofo,* the symbol of authority.

Each of Mazi Ejemba's friends lowered his head in a show of reverence as they all said, "Ezemmuo, mouthpiece of the gods, I greet you in fear of the gods."

Mazi Ejemba said, "May you live longer than your ancestors, Ezemmuo, the mouthpiece of the gods. Come and have a piece of kola nut."

Ezemmuo replied, "The toad does not run in the day for nothing. I have come with sackcloth to deliver the message from the gods. You have spoken ill of the goddess. Therefore, in four market days, you and your entire household shall be destroyed. Remember that the decisions of the gods are unquestionable." At this, he turned his back, trying to leave the compound.

"Is there anything that can be done, Ezemmuo?" asked Mazi Ejemba.

Ezemmuo cleared his throat. Speaking sadly, he said, "You have to appease the goddess. You will buy seven tubers of yam, twelve legs of cow, and a piece of land and offer them to Obianuju's father. Then, a fat white cow will be slaughtered in your house. Finally, you will dance round the village naked. This must be done within the next four market days, or else ..." He said all these sadly and went away whistling.

Since the authority of the gods is absolute, Mazi Ejemba had no option other than to fulfill the rites to appease the gods. He and his entire household could not withstand the calamity of death. Obianuju's parents received the gift from Ejemba with open hands. The legs of cows were sold in the market and earned them a lot of cowries. Obianuju's father used a part of the money to start a new business at Ofoala Trade Center, and her mother used hers to enrich her own business. Truly, the gods cracked their palm-kernels. They waited in hope for the next planting season, when they would plant maize and cassava on their new farmlands.

*   *   *

The entire household of Mazi Okenta was in conflict for two market days over their son's decision to marry Obianuju, a young girl from Osu family. Although Mazi Okenta has taken time to analyse the consequences of marrying an *Osu* to his son, Obidozie, yet his explanations fell on deaf ears.

Okenta, a successful farmer and a title holder well known throughout the clan and even beyond, cannot imagine his son bring disgrace to his family all in the name of love. He has used every measure even his wealth to convince his son not to marry Obianuju but all his efforts proved abortive. Okenta, therefore swore with his life to disown his son if he should marry Obianuju. Worst still, Uloma, Obidozie's mother, had already sworn to commit suicide if the marriage should continue.

Obidozie woke up at the middle of the night after sleepless night. While facing their thatched house built with bamboo and red mud, he was filled with the memories of previous night which he spent together with Obianuju and family. Tears started rolling down his cheeks as he recalls these memories. He could not withstand abandoning Obianuju in order to keep his family so-called honor. Worst still, despite the fact that he regarded his mother as his pearl, he could not abandon Obianuju. After recounting all these, he went outside his hut, sat down and was being kept company by the sounds of insects. Obidozie's thought that night was distracted by the sound of the flies and insects perching around his ear, and he often slapped himself while trying to kill them.

Umuabali is a remote village surrounded by bushes, rivers and forests. All these have effects on the living condition of the people. They have stagnant rivers where most unfriendly insects live. At times, dangerous animals come out of the forest, especially at night, to attack little children during their moonlight plays. Owing to this, most parents no longer allow their children to come out for the moonlight plays for security reasons.

An idea suddenly came to Obidozie's mind, he remembered his uncle Mazi Mbaneme, a man whom he takes as next to his father and one to whom he often come to take advice whenever he is confused. Mbaneme, just like Okosisi, is a title holder and also respected among the wise elders of the Igwe's Council of Elders. His great importance in the Council cannot be over emphasized as each meeting cannot yield much without him. His suggestions are usually decisive as he is endowed with wisdom from the god. But the only thing that belittles him is his lack of male child. In Igbo land and even beyond, male children are the pride of a man. One may possess all the titles, wealth and joys of this life, but without a male child, he may not be given all the respects he deserves. Obidozie had to wait patiently until the sunrise before he could begin his journey to the house of Mazi Mbaneme. While siting on the bamboo seat beside his father's hut, he supported himself with his hands on his cheek.

After a short while, he discovered a little sun ray, he stood up from his seat and cleared his throat twice, he poured three little drops of palm wine on the ground pouring libation, thanking the gods for giving him a bright morning and pleading for the protection of his life. He washed his face, hands and legs. He then went inside his hut, picked up his chewing stick and machete and started making his journey to the house of Mazi Mbaneme.

Obidozie is a good hunter who never misses his target. As he walked quietly he also watched so carefully, looking for a game.

His quiet mood was distracted by the whistling of a man coming in front of him. At first, he was angry because the noise will scare away the game, but when he watched carefully, he saw Ugonna his childhood friend with his little son walking towards him.

"Dozie, Dozie …" Ugonna called,

"Who am I seeing?" Obidozie asked.

They both exchanged pleasantries. Obidozie dropped his machete hugged him and said:

"Ugo",

"Yes my brother, it has been a very long time. But we thank the gods for keeping us alive till today."

"Yes", Obidozie said as he nodded his head.

"And whose child are you with?" asked Obidozie as he admires the little handsome boy.

"It's my son", he replied and continued.

"I am taking him round the village. It's his first time of being at his father's place."

"Really, that's good", he said and continued nodding his head.

"Little boy, what's your name?" he asked.

"My name is Mezie" the little boy replied. Obidozie was short of words, he continued starring at the boy and continued to wonder when he would have his own son who would bear his own name. In order not to make his ugly gestures noticed, Obidozie quickly ended the discussion and each of them departed.

Obidozie turned back and continued looking at Ugonna and his son Mezie until he could no longer see them. He looked up to the skies, tears filled his eyes and he began to question the gods why misfortune has preoccupied his life. At this point, he lost his patience. He therefore vowed to marry Obianuju even if it might cost his father disowning him or his mother's death. He lost the interest of continuing in the journey, but held his peace towards taking any action because he has to wait until the new yam festival, so that he might not defile himself before the gods.

Chapter 3

Most times, we seem to question the gods why misfortune comes to those who don't deserve it. We can see that it is the innocent who suffer gravely in our world while evil men thrive. Igwe Maduka falls under the category of the good men who suffer misfortune.

The gods created him with whatever a man of his status deserves, but whenever he remembers his son Dike, he tends to question the gods. Dike is evil. He is very notorious and this earned him much prominence. Of course, Igwe Maduka is aware of how dangerous his son was, but the old king keeps praying to the gods to make his son's life new.

It was very early in the morning, after the cock crow. Mazi Ugomba made his way to the Igwe's palace to meet with the Igwe and to narrate to him his ordeal.

"Ugo Igbo ji eje mba," Igwe Maduka called as soon as he saw Mazi Ugomba approaching his palace.

"I hope all is well,

Is there any problem?

Or have you come for peace?"

Too many questions were asked at the same time by the Igwe, and Ugomba never knew where to begin his story.

"Igwe, my son Nnabugo came back yesterday, with bruises all over him.

He was beaten up by your son Dike, who went to the market and ordered everyone to vacate the market place because the Crowned Prince of the land has arrived."

"You mean my son beat up your son for just his pride?" Igwe Maduka asked and was short of words. He did not seem to understand how Dike would order the people to vacate the market place because he arrived at the market.

Igwe Maduka was trying to plead with Mazi Ugomba when he heard the voice of a poor woman from afar crying and laying curses on the Prince - Dike. The woman was coming to the palace and was rolling herself on the ground.

Igwe Maduka was moved with pity. He stood up from his throne and held the woman and asked, "What is it woman?"

Tears couldn't allow the poor widow to speak.

"Your son, your son." she said, "went to the stream and ordered all those in the stream to leave. My daughter, Akwaugo, only bent down to fetch a pot of water and your son, Dike gave her a beating of her life. She came back yesterday with bruises all over her," she continued to lament.

The Igwe was disappointed. "It's alright woman, don't worry yourself any longer. Take your daughter to the herbalist and I will pay the bill, as for that evil son of mine, I will deal with him in my own way, please *biko*," Igwe Maduka calmly said to the woman.

The woman rose up, tightened her wrapper and went away. Igwe Maduka stood for some seconds and thought of what to do.

"Dike!, Dike!!, Dike!!!", his voice thundered.

"Yes Papa", Dike answered. He came into his father's Obi and looked into his father's eyes saying, "Papa, you called me".

"What did you do at the market yesterday?" Igwe Maduka asked.

"Hmm … Papa is that supposed to be a question? In the market I bought some items." Dike replied arrogantly.

"Mazi Ugomba here told me how you went to the market and ordered my people out of the market and so many people were beaten up", said Igwe.

"Yes, those were the people who refused to obey the royal order." He said.

"Shut up, you fool! Each time, I continue to remind you that you are just like your late mother, very proud and arrogant. What do you know about royalty? That was just the same way your late mother was before the vengeance of the gods caught up with her." Igwe Maduka said angrily.

"Papa I'm not a fool", Dike said.

"Look old man," he pointed at his father and said "Keep my late mother out of this,"

"And as for you" he turned to Mazi Ugomba,

"Don't think you have succeeded because you haven't. Just don't worry. We shall see," Dike left his father's Obi and went away.

"Dike, come back here", his father called.

He never listened to him and he went out of the compound.

Ugomba was very much disappointed.

"*Igwe, ka odibazie.* I will come back on *Nkwo* market day," Mazi Ugomba went away whistling.

Mazi Ugomba was strangled to death by some young boys on his way back from the Igwe's Palace.

Adaego and Nwabuaku, two maidens from Umuabali were coming back from the stream with their pots of water when they suddenly saw the dead body of Mazi Ugomba lying helpless beside the Ofoala Stream.

"*Chineke mee!!!*" they screamed and broke their pots of water. They ran into the village to alert the youths.

Agunwata, the great hunter who shoots without missing was the first person to come closer to the scene. It was a shock to him when he saw the corpse of his in-law lifeless and he carried the corpse to the village square. Egwuatu, the town crier alerted the people to come to the village square immediately. It was an *Afor* market day and some women had already gone to the farm, but the ugly sound of the *Udu* and *Ekwe* was so terrible that no one could neglect the call. It was a sound of danger and misfortune.

Ezemmuo came to the village square with disbelief. How can a man like Mazi Ugomba die such a shameful death? The question made him speechless. Worst still, the gods have refused to open up the cause of the death. Ezemmuo wanted to carry out an autopsy to find out the cause of Mazi Ugomba's death but Mazi Mbaneme came to him and whispered something to him and Ezemmuo nodded in agreement. Mbaneme had just told Ezemmuo that Mazi Ugomba took an Ozo title. According to their tradition, no autopsy should be carried out on the body of someone who had the Ozo title.

Ezemmuo cleared his throat twice and said,
"Our people say that,
When a child is crying and pointing
towards a direction, if his mother is not there,
then his father must be there.
Nothing, in this world is hidden under
the sun and the gods will hear us soon."

The people started murmuring and making some comments, when one of the elders stood up and said:

"Ezemmuo, we don't understand your proverbs."

The people concurred to what the elder has said because he spoke their mind.

"Which proverb do you not understand? Or is it that the bride-price paid on your mother's head is a waste?" Ezemmuo calmly said.

"This is the strangest incident I have ever seen since I was born. The gods have remained silent to this and I don't seem to understand. Mazi Ugomba will not be buried immediately. He will be buried on Eke market day. Special rites are to be performed for him not just because he took the Ozo title but because he is also Nwa Njoku and the 'Iwankita anya' rite will be performed before he will be buried" said Ezemmuo. The elders nodded in agreement.

Nwa Njoku is a person dedicated to *Njoku*, the deity responsible for fertility, especially yam crops, and such persons are their father's favourite sons. Such a person is sacrosanct. It is abomination to injure him. His head, at death never touches the ground, if it does, calamity of grave proportion befalls his extended family members.

Chapter 4

The African treasures are immanent in their customs and cultures. In Africa, there is wide and vast range of traditions, cultures and festivals that help in the identification of every race, tribe and clan. In Igbo land, the new yam festival has remained prominent over the years. Yam is considered as a supernatural food for the living and the dead. It is something amazing that while the living obviously eats yam meals, the dead equally demand for their share. It is an important festival among various other festivals celebrated. This festival was celebrated in honour of the gods, to thank them for good harvest. It is a period of thanksgiving, prayer, supplication and communion between friends, parents, brothers, sisters and in-laws. The ability to own several barns of yam is a mark of wealth, self-sufficiency and hard work. It provides the people the opportunity to thank Ahiajoku the yam deity for a successful farming season and ask for his help, benevolence and protection against misfortune.

Ahiajoku is the diety responsible for good yields, especially yam. Before yam is planted, certain rituals are performed. Even after the harvesting of yam and when it is stored in the barn, rituals are also performed to thank Ahiajoku for fertility. The origin of Ahiajoku, the yam deity is as old as yam itself. A story was told about how the son of *Ndri* died. After several years of his death, yam tendering started to grow from his grave. This incident greatly influenced the ownership of Ahiajoku spirit in Igbo land. One has to keep his hands clean while celebrating the new yam festival.

Ezemmuo, the Chief-Priest, has announced to the people about the new yam festival coming up on orie market day. But however, the people are to undergo a purification rite on *Eke* market day to prepare them and make them holy to appear before the gods.

The Igwe sent his town crier to go round the village and invite the elders of the council to an emergency meeting. With the sound of the gong, the attention of the people were drawn to the town crier, Egwuatu, a renowned analytic orator of the time.

"Listen, all wise elders of the Igwe's council. The Igwe has requested for your royal presence at his royal palace before noon, there is an important message from the oracle of the hills and caves," said Egwuatu the town crier.

No elder needed a soothsayer to tell him that the message is about the new yam festival that is fast approaching. They were aware of the good harvest *Ahiajoku* has already bestowed on them, they were equally aware of the new moon full at its peak.

The elders began to make their way to the Igwe's palace to answer the call from the king. Each holding his walking stick, dressed in their traditional attire, cap on their heads and beads across their necks. Mazi Ukaegbu,

19

one of the elders has already taken permission for his absence at the meeting. He sustained fracture the previous night while tapping palm wine. The orthopedist had recommended that his movement be restricted until the next planting season when he must have recovered fully.

The elders were already settled at the palace, yet the meeting could not commence. They were waiting for Mazi Mbaneme to arrive. Mbaneme is living seven kilometers away from the Igwe's palace, and he is not getting any younger as he could scarcely move. Yet the elders and the Igwe must await his arrival because of his wisdom and his well-known decisive suggestions. Finally, after a little period of time, Mbaneme managed to arrive the palace.

He greeted the Igwe in his usual words,

"May you live long my king," he bent slightly, exchanging greetings with him. He as well saluted the elders in the forum.

The Igwe then cleared his throat twice and said, "I thank you all my people for honouring my invitation. The oracle has formally pronounced the new yam festival coming up on Orie market day but we all must undergo a purification rite to make us holy to appear before the oracle of the hills and caves."

The Igwe also reminded the people of the taboo associated with the celebration of the festival. He cleared his throat and said, "My people do not forget the abominations one can commit against Ahiajoku, the yam deity. Remember that Ahiajoku forbids the indiscriminate throwing of yam tubers. No matter the sizes, yam tubers must be carried with dignity and respect. Ensure that you do not violate the Igbo farming calendar. Ahiajoku farming days must be observed. Remember that the yam barn must be kept neat before the yam is stored. Failure to observe this may lead to the disappearance of tubers of yam in the barns. Stealing is a taboo to Ahiajoku deity."

The Igwe continues, "The act of stealing yam, either in the farm, yam barns or anywhere is against *Ahiajoku*. Do not forget that the wrath of *Ahiajoku* over these offences could befall an individual offender, his kindred, village or community. The kindred may be stricken with infirmity, insanity, pestilence or poor harvest", the elders nodded in agreement with the king and stated that he has said it all. There were cheers and ovations when Mazi Mbaneme stood up to talk, and he said, "Igwe, your idea has been welcomed, but I suggest that the purification rite be done on the early morning of Orie market day. Do not forget that the corpse of our late brother Mazi Ugomba will be buried on Eke Market day and the hands of those who are to carry the corpse would be purified as well." This he said and gently sat down. The idea was found wonderful. The Igwe thanked him for his contribution and urged the elders to do it the way he suggested.

At sunrise, the villagers went to the house of Mazi Ugomba to pay him the last respect. He was found dead in a nearby bush, he was assassinated by Dike, the Prince. Some people believed that he was attacked by a wild animal, others also held the stand that he must have been stricken down by *Ezenwanyi Abali* (the Queen of the night) for killing the Queen's pet.

The truth was that Ugomba is dead and his body must not be allowed to be a feast for vultures. He has to be buried. Ezemmuo instructed that some valuables be buried alongside with him, such as his favourite dresses, walking stick and money, which he would use to pay his debts during his journey. He would be missed by the people. He had two sons and a daughter, including his wife, to mourn him. He died a painful death - truly his death is a misfortune.

"We cannot question the gods," said Ezemmuo at the scene of the funeral where most of the villagers were weeping and wailing. Ezemmuo cleared his throat and said, "Crying will neither solve the problem nor our weeping able to bring him back from the land of our ancestors. Let us therefore await the gods to fulfill their promises."

Mazi Ugomba was buried according to *Nwa Njoku* and *Iwa Nkita Anya* rites. The *Iwa Nkita Anya* rite involves killing a dog and pouring some of the blood into the eyes of the deceased, while lying in state. The dog used for this rite is usually provided by the Age Group to which the deceased belongs. The blood of the dog is poured directly into his pupil, which is the center of the eye. This is so because, Igbos believe that the blood, cleanses the pupil, and one whose pupil is cleansed becomes wiser than he was in his life time, and also as smart as a dog.

Mazi Ugomba was a man of valor who achieved so much in his life time and therefore should be identified as such in the spirit world. As the corpse arrived at the burial site, it was lowered into the grave, the grave was closed and all went sorrowfully away, leaving behind the poor widow and her three children.

Due to the nature of the death, Ezemmuo recommended that large quantity of grave food be put into his grave to provide comfort for him during his journey to the spirit world.

Africans believe that a man transfers his status to the spirit world. Men of importance and great achievements are therefore made to enter the spirit world with as much fanfare as possible, so that their identity would not be mistaken.

* * *

In Africa every sunrise is a story. On early hours of the day of the new yam festival, the drum was beaten, the drum that awakes the sun. Little children came out with their popular song - 'itempe', a song of early morning rise. They were singing loudly and their voices were heard wide. The chief priest, Ezemmuo, rebuked them and asked them to stop.

"We are just about to observe the purification rite and you are already singing and dancing. Abomination!!! Children of this generation, you are yet to tell us what you people will turn out to be", Ezemmuo said as silence filled the entire scene of the purification. Old women and maidens came for the atonement of their sins, to make them apparently holy before the gods. After the sacrifices, the people then began to sing and dance. It was really a happy scene and the people were already eating and drinking with lots of fun and amusement.

Soon after the ceremony started, the unexpected happened. A warrior from Ozoala clan was hired by Dike to assassinate the Igwe. At first, he disguised himself as a lover and well-wisher of Umuabali people, who has come to witness their festival. Later, he hid himself behind the big 'apu' tree that was about 100 meters away from the scene of the festival. From there he shot his arrow at the forehead of the Igwe which finally pierced into his head and he died.

The happy mood of the entire community was suddenly turned into a scene of commotion and turmoil. Tears, screams and whaling of the people were heard even by those in the neighboring communities. It was really a significant coincidence, the people were left with mixed feelings and the following questions remained unanswered: Why must Ahiajoku the yam deity allow such misfortune to befall the people on a special celebration like this? Does it mean that the sacrifices offered by the people are all wastes? Do the people really have gods and ancestors as they claim and if they have, why must their gods and ancestors fold their hands and watch their defeat and downfall? Are their gods angry with them or has the Igwe soiled his hands with blood?" - All these constituted the pending questions. But who is in the best position to answer them?

Twenty-one market days of mourning was declared by Ezemmuo, the chief priest, following the death of Igwe.

The corpse of the late Igwe would he carried across the seven rivers of Umunneoma as customary, where he would be deified. Ugoeze, the Igwe's wife, shall scrape off her hair and put on a black robe as custom also demands, her food must be cooked separately from that of the children, just as the gods strictly instructed. Adaeze, Igwe's first daughter, shall carry her father's image around the nine clans of Umuabali Kingdom, and finally dance round her father's corpse, thus paying him the last respect.

"O! The day of the people of Umuabali has gone dark. The great Iroko tree, the pride of Umuabali has fallen. The Igwe is no more. Yes! The gods are not to be blamed. Ozoala people have broken our hearts and shattered us with a single bow and arrow of a successful and professional warrior" Ezemmuo exclaimed. "What do we do next?" he continued, "We shall not go to war, of course, we are still mourning; no other decision shall be taken until the twenty-one market are over."

Chapter 5

Two market days have passed since the death of the Igwe. His son Dike asked the palace guard to send for Egwuatu the town crier. Egwuatu hesitated in his coming because he had visitors from a distant land and could not abandon them to answer the call. His in- laws from Alaoma had just visited him to see how their family have been doing. He presented kolanuts to them as a sign of hospitality. Egwuatu asked them about Alaoma, and they answered by enumerating the successes of their clan since last planting season, and how the gods have continued to shower them with bountiful harvest.

His in-laws later asked him about his people. Egwuatu remained calm for some minutes, took a calabash of palm wine, drank it and poured away the remaining while murmuring.

"Nothing good has ever come here," he threw the calabash away and cleared his throat.

"Our Igwe joined his ancestors two market days ago" he said soberly.

"Ewoo! Chai!!" they exclaimed.

"That man was a good leader. I can vividly remember how he treated us with respect and humility on the day you paid our sister's bride price," one of the men said.

"We shall miss him so much. Our prayer is that we should have someone like him as our Igwe and not that evil son of his."

He was still speaking when he saw a group of palace guards entering his compound. He rebuked the guards for coming out because the tradition has it that movement out of the palace should be restricted in cases of death. He kept calm when he noticed the presence of the prince.

"My Prince, is everything alright?" Egwuatu asked.

"I sent a message across to you to come to the palace and you flattened my royal orders, right?

Egwuatu wanted to explain but Dike gave him a slap. He kept quiet and felt embarrassed.

Dike ordered the palace guards to beat him and Egwuatu was beaten, flogged mercilessly, dragged to the mud and treated like a criminal.

Dike immediately left the compound for Ezemmuo's shrine. He arrived at the shrine and walked in without respect. "What is the matter, my Prince?" Ezemmuo asked furiously.

"Two market days have passed since my father's death, yet I have not heard any word from you, concerning my coronation." Dike said.

"Abomination! Speak not my dear child,
Your father's corpse is still lying helpless,
He has been defeated by his rivals,

Why do you speak of coronation too soon?
Or have you long awaited his death?" Ezemmuo said.

"No, may the gods forbid. I have never thought of that.
I am not here for dialogue,
I am here to tell you to coronate me,
as soon as possible", Dike replied.

"I must hear from the gods before you will be coroneted.
The gods are silent. Be patient, until the gods speak",
Ezemmuo said.

"For your information,
I will be coroneted in two market days.
And you cannot do anything to stop that" said Dike.
Ezemmuo started laughing and asked,
"Who will give you the *Ofo,*
the staff of leadership?"

This statement made Dike very much angry. He could not send his guards to beat up Ezemmuo because he knew how grievous it is to touch a messenger of the gods. He went away angrily.

Ofo is the symbol of authority and it is sacred. It is the source of the Igwe's legal power and a medium of relationship between him and his ancestors. There is no king without the *Ofo* and Dike was very much aware of this. He was restless all through the night and did not know what to do. He left his father's palace at mid-night to the shrine. Ezemmuo was not in the shrine at that moment, but he saw Oduche, Ezemmuo's servant.

"My Prince, what do you seek at this time of the night?" Oduche asked anxiously. "Keep quiet! Come here!!!" Dike ordered.

Oduche came closer fearfully. Dike grabbed him at the throat and killed him. Dike desecrated the shrine and stole the *Ofo* from the shrine.

Early in the morning, Dike went to the houses of some of the elders and paid them fifty cowries each to support his coronation. Egwuatu, the town crier was immediately sent to inform the villagers to gather at the village square at noon.

Dike was coroneted with a stolen *Ofo* in the absence of Ezemmuo, and thus, no ritual was performed at his coronation.

Chapter 6

Dike's coronation was the beginning of misfortune in Umuabali. Their farm animals were dying on daily bases. Ofoala stream suddenly dried up and for about seven market days, the sky refused to send down the rains. Pregnant women now die at the process of childbirth and worst still, the soil, which has been fertile, suddenly lost its fertility. The villagers were in fear as none could be able to speak out for them.

The elders refused to be swept under the carpet and set out for a journey to the Igwe's palace at sunrise, on the early hours of Orie market day. Each of them came up to him with his own part of the story and account of the ugly events. Mazi Nzekwe was the first to enter the palace followed by the other elders.

"May you live long my king", each greeted and tried to give a slight bow. The Igwe responded and welcomed them to his palace.

"My king", Ogbonna began and cleared his throat. "The toad does not run in the daytime for nothing sake. We, the members of your cabinet, have come to search for the black goat in the daytime, for at night it will be difficult".

"Hmm…I see, and if I may ask, which of your black goats is missing?", he asked jokingly.

"Igwe, not really. We have come to bring to your notice the strange things that have been happening in this village, ranging from the death of our farm animals, our pregnant women and children; the infertility of our soils, and drought caused by the absence of rain. We hope you are aware of these", Mbaneme added. The elders nodded in agreement because Mbaneme has spoken their mind.

The Igwe nodded his head and cleared his throat twice saying, "The clearing of the throat as you all know is a means of paving way for men, the spirits and the gods to hear you speak. Hold your ears now, whatever that happens in my land is my own responsibility and no one has the right to question me. Leave me to solve my own problem the way I want. I am Igwe and as you all know, my name is Dike which implies that I am great. I am a man and can solve my own problems when the time comes."

"When will the time come, is it when we all end up dead?" the elders asked angrily.

"I think I am done with you. Now, leave my palace", the elders looked at one another and went away accordingly.

The situation of things grew worst and no attempt to solve the problem was made by the Igwe. He keeps on telling the people that he will solve the problem in his own way and in fact, he is on top of the situation.

One day, there was an outcry from a nearby home. The voice of a young girl was heard from afar. The people gathered and asked, *"O bu gini? What is it?"* She could not respond but was only able to point at the corpse of her aging mother and her three sisters lying on the floor. They

31

had come back from the farm and ate a freshly prepared *Ugba* delicacy and after an hour or more they died. This was really strange. *Ugba* is an African salad and was eaten by the people on special occasions. But is anything wrong with the *Ugba* this family had eaten that had wiped them away?

Egwuatu, the town crier went round the village to call the elders for an emergency meeting, "gom, gom, gom, gom, gom" was the sound of his *Ogene*. "All the men, women and children of Umuabali are expected to gather at the village square before sunset today for urgent matters to be deliberated, gom, gom," he went to another direction to spread his message.

That evening, the villagers gathered at the village square. Mazi Ogbonna was the first to speak. "Our people say that so many words are not fitting for daybreak. We are all aware of the calamities that have befallen us and we have come to find solution to our problems."

The people nodded in agreement and after a long time of deliberation, Mazi Mbaneme came up with an idea. Standing up gently he said, "the gods of our land have remained silent of this issue. Let us now send some men to Umuaku, I know a strong Dibia-afa who can give us the solution to the problem."

"That is a wonderful Idea", The elders concurred. Three men were sent to Umuaku the following morning to meet with the Priestess of Umuaku who serve Amadioha, the god of thunder.

Meanwhile, the Priestess was aware of their coming and did not allow them to speak nor enter her shrine, "you evil people, who collect bribe from the Prince to win the fortune of money. Now you have crowned the wrong one and the gods are out for you. You shall continue to suffer until the gods speak", she regrettably said. Wise one, we are sorry for our action, can anything be done?", one of the messengers retorted.

"Your Igwe has soiled the land and desecrated the shrine. He spilt the blood of Oduche all over the land. That child's blood is crying and can never be comforted. He stole away the *Ofo*, the symbol of authority out of the shrine. Oh, he deserves to die!!!" She assured.

The Priestess left her shrine immediately and made her way to Umuabali, to the palace of Dike. She was known for her outspokenness and brevity.

"Dike, Dike", she called as her voice thundered.

"Your calabash has over flown with the blood of the innocent and the blood has spilt all over our land. Their voices can be heard but never comforted", she said and continued,

"Now, you must confess to your people all you have done and dance round the village naked. This must be done before sunset tomorrow", she said and left the palace. "Ezenwanyi", Dike called.

"I have always served the gods with my whole heart and I have not offended the gods in any way".

"...before sunset tomorrow, before sunset tomorrow," the priestess continued to emphasis this until she got back to Umuaku, the neighboring village. Dike did not obey the Priestess. At midnight, he was struck by *Amadioha*, the gods of thunder. The vultures and dogs came to eat his body. That was the end of Dike. Immediately, the *Ofo* disappeared into the forest.

Chapter 7

Obidozie also shared in the grievance of his people. As a man of peace he had always said in discussions that he would not desire to go into war with the Ozoala people, but if that is the only way he could demonstrate his love for his people, then he would. He has undergone several gestures in his decision to marry an Obianuju from his family and friends. Reasonable number of people who claimed to be soothsayers has visited him in his hut telling him how a young girl has blinded him just to win the fortune of marriage from him. Yes, these so called soothsayers has allegiance with Obidozie's father who paid them thirty cowries to convince his son not to marry Obianuju. However, in his steadfastness he has proved the validity of the popular adage, "Love is blind". Amidst all these, someone seems to be saying the truth that the union between Obianuju and Obidozie is a union from the gods. Their destiny might be delayed, but above all it cannot be denied. Most at times or often, the decisions we take do not seem to be what we uphold, hence the gods have their own way of doing things.

Obianuju left home after sunset for the moonlight play at the village square where most of her peers have come, to rest their nerves after the fatigue of their daily work. Young girls in their early teens trooped in groups to the venue with a piece of cloth tied round their breast and beads across their waist. Their faces were painted with *nzu*, clear and delible enough to produce best results. Across their neck were beads worn parallel to each other. At that very night, information was passed across to the Chief Priest from the land of the Ancestor that the soul of the Igwe shall not be at rest until the *ofo* is returned from the forest and the next Igwe be installed. Besides, the gods have given only four market weeks to provide it, or else calamity will befall our land.

There was a sudden uproar from the crowd. Ojiofor, son of Mazi Ogumba asked, "Has the gods selected some men who shall go to the forest and return the *ofo*". It was then that Ezemmuo bent down with his eyes closed and randomly pointed out seven men out of the crowd. Amadi's son Nwamadi, Onyeneke son of Oparaji, Nnaemeka son of Kamalu, Ibe son of Mazi Ogbuji, Oguzie son of Ugorji, Uche son of Nze Okafor and Obidozie son of Mazi Okenta. They were to set out for the journey at sunrise to the forest, and meanwhile, Ezemmuo, the Chief Priest, had earlier informed them that their journey is a matter of life and death. However, there is a prize for anyone who must return with the *ofo* alive. Anyone who comes back with the ofo alive shall automatically be installed the next Igwe of Umuabali.

Obianuju received the news about Obidozie's selection to the forest with a great shock. At first, she couldn't believe it until Obidozie came up to her and told her everything. She was filled with sorrow.

"Why me... why me ..." She lamented, "why must the gods allow such misfortune to befall me?, why must the gods select mine?"

Obidozie consoled and assured her that he was to live for her and for the sake of the entire people. "Do not cry Obianuju, I will always live for you and for my people, I see this as a way the gods have chosen to bring us fortune", he advised.

He then began to sing for her to feel relieved,

"Obi mu ooo, Ifunanya mu ooo. odim n'obi, mu na gi ga-ebi."

Tears began to roll down the cheeks of the poor girl.

Obianuju is a woman of great prestige and admiration. She appears outstanding among her peers and that is the quality that makes most of her peers to be always jealous of her. She is simply different. In fact, she is a typical example of an ideal African-igbo woman.

At sunset, Ezemmuo called the seven youths together at his shrine and presented them before the gods. They do not need to be purified again because they were purified during the new yam festival. He breathed upon them and instructed them to open their hands, he painted *nzu* at the centre of their palms and gave them power over minor deities and spirits. He instructed them of the necessity to treat every creature in the forests with dignity and respect, and equally advised them to make the journey in the daylight and rest at night after the fatigue of their daily work.

"It is necessary for you to rest at night. This is to help you to make a good result at dawn." He adviced.

He prayed for them and sent them forth in peace.

"Be united" he said, "it will always help you to succeed".

They waited patiently for the dawn, and at dawn, they set out for the journey -A journey of life and death.

Chapter 8

The seven warriors of Umuabali started their journey on the first day. The journey was full of fun and amusement. Nweke, the great comedian was there to entertain them with his jokes. Obidozie has not walked such a great distance before, although he enjoys travelling as his hobby. The warriors looked fierce and threatening that most of the people who saw them ran away.

On reaching Ozoala market, the people in the market saw them and fled and informed their kinsmen that Umuabali people have sent some youths to wage war against them. Ozoala people have for long proved to be natural enemies of the people of Umuabali, on the contrary Umuabali people have nothing against them.

The Ozoala people are envious of Umuabali people because of the Ekeogu Market that has remained prominent over the years. The fertility of their land was another point of emphasis and the oil that has currently been discovered on Umuabali soil. As the Ozoala people target to start a war, yet the gods of the land continued to bless the people of Umuabali.

A story was told of how Dikeogu, the gods of war deserted the people of Ozoala. The warriors of Ozoala people once went to war and defeated their enemies and had them as slaves. When they came back, instead of giving thanks to their gods for their success, they rather attributed all the glory to themselves, and the gods of war deserted them. Since then they have never gone to war and succeeded.

For several years, Umuabali has received numerous threats from the Ozoala people. They wish to begin a war, conquer them and have them as slaves; have their market, and receive payments for the oil found in their land.

The warriors crossed the seven rivers of Aroigwe before they finally arrived the mighty forest. It was a difficult task trying to find out the route that led to the forest because all the entrances looked alike. It was then that they realized that the journey has just begun. They looked up to the sky and could not imagine what they were seeing - blood in the sky.

Suddenly, there appeared a strange being behind them with long hairs, long fingers and toes. He is the prince of the forest, he meant no harm. He is a loving spirit and he loves wrestling with humans after which he would come to their help.

Nnaemeka was so bold to walk up to the prince of the forest and said, "wise one, we are warriors from the land of Umuabali, sent by our Chief Priest to get the ofo from the forest, for our late Igwe whose soul is still wondering all over the land helpless. We have missed our way and we need your help".

"Hmm..." his voice thundered,

"Did I hear you say warriors?"

"Yes ..." replied Nnaemeka.

"One of you should wrestle with me", he said while laughing.

The warriors looked at themselves to see who would go into wrestling match with the prince. Nnaemeka then stepped aside and came nearer to him and said, "I will wrestle with you."

"Ha ha ha", the prince laughed.

"I love your boldness" he said and pulled his robe, untied his sandals and cattle skin belt, stepped out, and got ready for the wrestling.

Nweke brought out his flute and began to blow it. The wrestling match began.

The Prince crossed his legs and folded Nnaemeka's arm, pulled him up and allowed him to land-crash. Nnaemeka shouted with a loud voice, the other warriors ran to him to help him and asked him to rise and continue to wrestle. He stood up. Nweke picked up his flute and continued to blow it. Nnaemeka bounced back and pulled his whole weight towards the prince and fell upon him. They both were on the floor struggling when the prince pushed him with his feet and Nnaemeka fell on the ground helpless. The prince walked towards him, held him by his hand and said:

"That was wonderful, poor warrior", he helped him up and shook hands with him.

"Who are you?" Nnaemeka asked.

"I am the prince of the forest, son of Dikeogu the gods of war. I have lived in the forest for centuries all alone, being kept company by forest trees. I can walk around the forest in some minutes, but it will take you mortals several days to do just that. That is what makes us different. I love wrestling and I wrestle even with mortals like you before I can offer them help", he said and began to laugh.

"Well then, we need you to show us the direction of how to find the Ofo", Nnaemeka pleaded.

"The Ofo...oh the Ofo, follow here and walk straight. When you get to that junction, take the left path and continue going, you will find the ofo. It has been there waiting for you for days. Go, for your own good and for the good of your people. You shall find the Ofo hanging in the basket. I bet you, not all of you will make the journey. Ha, ha. ha ...", he laughed and disappeared. The warriors were perplexed by those words and they set out for the journey speechless.

*   *   *

Obianuju refused to taste anything since Obidozie left for the forest. She poured away her meal in the morning and pretended as if she had eaten them. At noon she locked herself up in her hut and refused to eat the food which her mother prepared.

"Obianuju, Obianuju," her mother called.

"Yes Mama", she replied and walked towards her mother facing the sun.

"Your food is ready", she said.

"Mama, am not hungry," Obianuju replied.

The mother walked up to her. Looking into her eyes she asked, "*Nwa m, o bu gini*? Talk to me I am your mother."

Obianuju finally opened up, "Mama, its Obidozie. Am afraid something must have happened to him."

41

"O nwam, nothing will happen to him," her mother said.

"Eat your food, his destiny is in the hands of the gods," she advised.

Obianuju nodded and carried her pounded yarn. She picked up a ball and dipped it into the bowl of *Egwusi* soup and ate as her mother watches with admiration. Just like an ideal African woman, Obianuju finds it difficult to forget so easily the love she shared with Obidozie. She began to avoid the gathering of the maidens on Nkwo market days because at such gatherings, some of the maidens do turn it into an occasion of mockery at Obianuju over the selection of Obidozie for the forest. As a result, Obianuju preferred to be indoors in order to avoid people reminding her of that ordeal.

On certain occasions, whenever she wants to go to the river to fetch water, she would follow another route which was farer and narrow; but like a light she could not be hidden. It appears that the more she intended to run away from the maidens the more they draw closer to her. At the river, she joined the company of other maidens who missed her and were anxious about her sudden absence.

"Obianuju, we have not been seeing you for the past three market days," said Amaka. "Really?" Obianuju replied as she tries to put a smile on her face.

"Come on Obianuju, tell us what the problem is", said Chioma.

"Do not pretend as if everything is alright, or have you forgotten that we are your friends?" Nneka intervened.

Obianuju then calmed down and told them a big lie, "I visited Umunneoma my maternal home to see my mother's people" she said, and tried to give them some happy gestures; yet it was well known to the three maidens that all is not well but they did not want to inquire further.

They left at the same time, Obianuju was not able to tell them that she wanted to follow the other route, she therefore walked in their midst in order to hide herself from people whom she would not like to see. They were carrying their pots of water on their head. *Nzu* was used to decorate their bodies especially their foreheads, beneath their breasts, their arms and lips. *Ichaka* was tied across their feet and makes some sound at every step they take. Every man who passed across them must be compelled to look at them twice.

The gathering of the maidens were most at times referred as 'the line and kingdom of beauty', because it seems they all were selected and brought under one association. The reverse is the case because, every daughter of Umuabali is automatically a bonafide member of the maidens. Hence, we shouldn't be so surprise at their beauty because black is beautiful. A story was told that white men were attracted to Africa as a result of the beauty of the African woman. Most Africans believe that the gods took their time and best skills while creating the African woman. Little wonder why African women are cheerful, gorgeous, attractive and fascinating.

At special occasions, they look so beautiful like the River goddess, such that if you are not very careful you may liken them as one. At moonlight plays, the maidens entertain people with their dances. Most times, the male flocks choose their wives from the one who dances best. We were told that if there is anything that an African woman cannot do, it then implies that no other woman in the world can do it. In dancing, African women take the lead. In cooking they appear to be the best, but amidst all these good qualities, they have their own faults, of course like human beings, they must not perfectly be seen as angels. Yes, they are angels but special type of angels - Angels that eat beans.

Chapter 9

This was the third nightfall since the warriors of Umuabali began their journey to the forest. The sun was gradually setting and darkness was drawing nearer. The cracking of the frogs became unbearable and terrifying. Most of these frogs must have lived there for a very long period of time. The seven warriors of Umuabali are sorting for a place to spend the night after the fatigue of their daily work. Ezemmuo the chief priest had formally told them to do most of their works in the day and rest at night. However, he had also informed them that if they must sleep at night, then they must sleep like dogs, calm but vigilant. Previously, they had decided to sleep under the Orji tree but while they were about to settle down, they were chased away by three big snakes; one from the upper side of the tree and two from the left and right directions. Nweke boldly drew up his matchet to strike the snake, but the other Warriors shouted at him reminding him of what Ezemmuo had said concerning treating every creature in the forest with dignity and respect.

"Nweke, flee! Do not attack them", Nwamadi stressed.

"They are spirits, treat them with dignity", Nnaemeka advised.

"Do not worry", Nweke said "Watch me; I shall be very much careful."

Nweke then proceeded boldly to attack the snakes. Little did he know that a snake was at his back, he was struck at the neck by the snake, and the other warriors ran away trembling. Nweke was left alone, dying silently. The forest vultures were already waiting; they began to eat him up while he was still struggling to survive. Nweke did not survive the attack, and hence he died like a dog.

It is true that a tree does not make a forest but yet a forest can be influenced by a tree. The Orji tree surpasses every other tree in the forest, with its branches wide spread, birds make their shelter on the tree. A story was told of how *Opara-Oye*, the son of *Oye* refused to render services to his father but instead turned himself into a tree. Yes, the son of the great gods turned himself into a tree so that he may not render services to his father. This story is usually attributed to children by their parents to show them what laziness can do. The snakes on the tree were minor deities. Truly, Nweke can be likened to the little bird *Nza* who after eating its meal came up to challenge his *Chi* to a wrestling match. No mortal dare attack the gods and live to boast of it.

The warriors mourned the death of Nweke that night after they had settled under an Egbu tree. Before they settled down, they looked around to see if they could see any snake around because it is said that when a child is beaten by a bee, he begins to be terrified when he sees a housefly.

Obidozie was restless, he kept on remembering the incident that happened and he wished that Nweke would have listened.

"Well, that is the fate of a disobedient friend" he said and sighed. He tried to close his eyes to sleep but all his effort proved abortive. He kept on dreaming that he began speaking even while dreaming. This continued until Nnaemeka tapped him and he regained his consciousness. They made fun of him.

"It is morning already," Obidozie slightly said. After a short while, they heard the cock crow. They washed their faces and feet and thanked the gods for a bright morning, they poured libation to the gods and pleaded for a fortunate day and of course the gods are pleased with lawful sacrifices.

They set out for the journey at sunrise.

Obidozie sat down on dry grass with his feet crossed beneath his tighs and laid his head on the root of a tree. The sun was up and he had already exhausted his strength.

"Come up, Obidozie. The journey is still far", Nwarnadi stressed. Obidozie stirred at him from head to toe and sighed.

"It is very early for you to get tired so Soon", the others intervened as one of them stretched out his hand to draw him up. Obidozie shunned the request and closed his eyes slightly to take a nap, then he fell asleep.

Meanwhile, Obianuju was at home sweeping the compound and at the same time having feelings of sorrow in her heart, tears began to run down her cheeks, but she tried to control it. She then began to sing the love song *'Ifunanya'* a song she sang with Obidozie after their engagement at *Inyi* River. It appears that the more she tries to control the tears, the greater ones roll down. Obidozie felt very much relieved at this moment, he suddenly rose up from his slumber picked up his matchet and joined the other warriors. They felt perplexed on how he suddenly had a change and renewal of strength. The journey began earnestly.

On their arrival to the stream, they heard the voice of a woman calling for help. He was frightened and was trembling in fear. He boldly drew up his matchet and came closer to see. It was a pregnant woman seeking for someone to help her draw water from the stream. Little did he know that the pregnant woman was a forest witch. Nwamadi helped her with her water and stretched out his hands to help her stand, immediately she touched him, they both disappeared.

The other warriors waited so long for him and he couldn't come hack. They then decided to go to the stream to see things for themselves. On their way, one of their ancestors appeared to them and said.

"Do not go in search of him, for your search will only be in vain. He has treaded the path of the dead. Go and have your rest and continue your journey at sunrise. The journey is still far."

They left the scene.

Chapter 10

When the sun arose, the warriors woke up from their slumber, thanked the gods for the bright morning and asked for the repose of the souls of their brothers. They washed their hands, feet and their faces and were ready to set out for the journey. Onyeneke stayed back and refused to go with them, "come on Onyeneke, we are already late" Obidozie said loudly.

"You mean I should go with you?" he laughed.

"I am not ready to die, you people can go" he said angrily, "what is the meaning of that?" Oguzie asked.

"I said I am no longer comfortable with your journey, I am going home", Onyeneke said and wanted to leave.

"No!" Nnaemeka intervened, "that's not possible."

"Is the possibility all you need?" he turned and was determined to go.

"Let him go! He has chosen his own part" Obidozie boldly said. Onyeneke waved and turned back running to get back home. With his arrows and matchet, he was determined to deal with any creature that should stand on his way. He passed several trees and journeyed so long. At a point, he became very hungry and began to look up the trees if he could find fruits to eat. As he continued to search he saw Nwamadi up an *apu* tree, eating *apu*.

Nwamadi died when the pregnant woman touched him at the stream. A minor deity turned himself into Nwamadi, a familiar person to Onyeneke to use that means to attract Onyeneke.

"Nwamadi is that you?", Onyeneke asked.

"Yeah, I am the one", he answered and continued to eat his *apu*.

"We thought you were dead", he said.

"Dead?", he laughed "Don't mind those fools."

"How can I be dead, look at me, do I look dead?"

"of course you don't" Onyeneke replied.

'I am tired of this journey, I am going home! Thanks to the gods that I have seen you' he said.

"You made a nice choice... they may all end up dead" Nwamadi laughed.

"what are you eating?, am hungry" Onyeneke asked "just some *apu* fruits, do you care for some?"

"Of course I do", Onyeneke quickly replied.

Nwamadi gave some to him, and he ate.

"Do you care for more?", Nwamadi asked.

"No I don't, I am not feeling fine", Onyeneke said.

"Ha, ha, ha …" Nwamadi laughed.

Onyeneke fell on the ground and died.

That was the end of the stubborn fly.

*   *   *

The elders of Umuabali came up to the village square on an Eke market day. They were worried about the warriors they had sent to the forest for the past three market weeks. The gods had instructed that the *ofo* should be brought back before the fourth market week and the new Igwe installed immediately.

They therefore sent words to Ezemmuo and summoned him to the gathering of the elders. Ezemmuo arrived the village square asking, "what do you seek from me?"

"Ezemmuo, mouth piece of the gods, may you live long," Mazi Uzoukwu said. Clearing his throat, he continued, "Our people say that when a child is crying and pointing towards a direction, if his father is not there, his mother is. Ezemmuo, we want to know what has become of the warriors we sent to the forest."

"Ezemmuo, the market weeks are almost over and we are yet to hear from our warriors, I hope we are safe?" Mazi Okoro asked.

"I am only a mortal as you are, but the difference is that I speak what the gods ask me to say. As a mortal, I do not see the land of the dead. But one thing I believe is that their destiny lies in the hands of the gods. Last night while I was having some incantations, the gods revealed to me that there are only three warriors remaining. They are Nnaemeka, Oguzie and Obidozie and before the next two market days, the gods of our land will lead them back", Ezemmuo said. "You mean out of the seven warriors we sent only three are remaining?" Mbaneme asked.

"Their journey is a journey of life and death", Ezemmuo retorted, "This is the more reason why we must reward anyone who comes back with the *Ofo* alive. He will be installed the Igwe and also be allowed to choose a wife among the maidens," he continued.

Mazi Amadi could not believe what the Ezemmuo had said. "Ezemmuo, what of my son Nwamadi?, what has become of him?"

"Amadi ... let the dead bury the dead!", Ezemmuo said and left the village square whistling.

Amadi threw himself on the mud and was filled with sorrow, "my only son" he cried out. "Ezemmuo, you sent my only son to the forest to be eaten by the forest vultures, only to tell me let the dead bury the dead. Ezemmuo ... where is my son?" he cried aloud.

"Amadi, put yourself together".

"Take heart, Amadi"

"This is not the end of the world"

"The gods of our land will always be with you."

These were the words of the elders to Amadi in condolence over the death of his son.

Chapter 11

Ekeogu market is more prominent than the other markets in Umuabali kingdom and even beyond. It is situated at the centre of the village and attracts hundreds of people even those from the neighboring kingdoms. It was a popular market where buying and selling takes place on every Eke market day. Different food stuffs and fruits are sold in the market at cheap rates. The villagers begin the sales in the evening and end very late at night. Deferent myths and folk tales are told concerning the market, but the strangest amongst them is that at mid-night, the daughter of a river goddess comes to the market. After buying and selling, the people usually find the market clean and well kept the next day. Meanwhile, the mmpeople living around the market testify that they usually hear the sound of the drums, flutes and gongs at mid-night.

In Ekeogu market, there is a mighty tree which is taller than all other trees. It has broad branches on which birds make their nest and even lay eggs. The people sell under this tree because it gives shade and cools the environment. The tree has been there for so long, even the time of their ancestors. It is believed that it holds the life and destiny of most of the villagers, as some elders of the village pour libations at the foot of the tree paving way for their success and progress in life.

The question of who planted the tree has been a puzzle for centuries. Some strongly believe that the tree was planted by Ahiajoku, the yam deity and the gods of fertility as sign of the fertility of the land of Umuabali. Sometime ago, three youths who were not aware of the strangeness of the tree once decided to cut down the tree for firewood, but they were surprise with what they saw. At each strike they made against the tree, they witnessed blood oozing out from the bark of the tree. They ran away with fear. The following morning, news went round the village that the three youths were strangled to death at midnight in a cold blood. Since then, no one dares attempt cutting down the tree.

One *Eke* market day while the people were buying and selling in the market, the tree was struck down by thunder and it fell on the people, and killed so many of them. The news went round the village like wide fire as people ran towards the scene of the incident. There were outcry and whaling of the people. It was a heavy attack. Many people died and others were injured. It was unfortunate that Uloma, Obidozie's mother was at the scene of the incident. She died as well. Mazi Okenta and his household wept. Some people were not able to discover the corpse of their relatives because of the harm that was done on them. Mazi Egwuatu's daughter Ijeoma was so unlucky. She had finished selling for the day and was about to go when a woman called her back to convey a message. As she was listening to the woman, the storm struck the tree and it fell on them and they died. It was a great tragedy for the people of Umuabali. A question was resounding in their hearts, 'Is this the beginning of the vengeance of the gods?"

When Obianuju heard about the death of Obidozie's mother, she wept heavily, as one without hope. The silence of the cold hand of death was felt all over the village. The massive death attracted the attention of some white missionaries who sailed from Ireland to Africa. The white men felt it was time to teach the Africans about their new God. Umunneoma was the first place the white men arrived and had already started making converts, baptizing in the name of their God.

Obianuju's sorrow increased day by day. For her, suicide is the only answer to her problems. She has refused to eat or talk to anyone. Her father, Mazi Okosisi therefore thought it wise to send Obianuju to Umunneoma, her maternal home to live for sometime until things begin to get well.

Obianuju obeyed her parents and went to Umunneoma village. After some days she felt relieved with the company of her best friend, Ngozika (a young girl of her contemporary who is well behaved like Obianuju.) Of course it is said that birds of the same feather flock together.

Ngozika was among the few converts of the white men and she follows the white man's ways. One evening she came to Obianju and asked for a request, "Obianju" she called "I have something important to tell you. I think it's time I invite you to join my new faith." Obianuju was surprise at these words and asked "What do you mean?"

Ngozika cleared her throat and said, "Two market weeks ago, some white missionaries came to our land and spoke to us about their new God. *Nwanne m*, we saw wonders with our eyes and now I have come to believe."

"what did you believe?" Obianuju asked.

"Hmm … I have come to believe that the worship of our gods are all fetish," Ngozika said boldly.

"Stop! do not speak against the gods" Obianju retorted.

"Which gods, those carved woods? Our people have denounced them. And the white men burnt them into ashes.

"Ah!" Obianuju exclaimed, "I do not wish to be part of this discussion."

She folded her arms and did not speak again. Her eyes were red, like the eyes of a rat caught by the tail. She was truly annoyed with Ngozika because she knows how grievous it is for someone to speak against the gods. She slept very early at day break. She slept outside her hut because the moon was bright, with log of fire very close to her mat which made her warm because the harmattan wind was blowing heavily. She could hear the sound of the flute wearing in and out and the drums beaten by the children in the neighbouring compound who came out for the moonlight play.

Chapter 12

Obianuju ran out of her hut, holding tight to her wrapper. She went into the nearby hut with her calabash to draw water from her pot to quench her all night thirst. She dipped her hand inside her pot and the pot was empty. She sighed.

"Who must have emptied my pot?" she said to herself.

It was then that she remembered using the water for her chores the previous night. She picked up her pot and started making her way to Uzoakoli River to fetch water. She was surprise that she never met anyone on her way while going to the river, "perhaps, I am the only one with an empty pot today," she said to herself. She got to the river and fetched her water. She carried the pot of water on her head and started making her way back home.

Two women were coming before her; they were the *Umuada* of Umunneoma village. "Good morning," Obianuju greeted.

"Young girl, where are you coming from?" one of the women asked, holding tight to her wrapper and standing with her hand on her waist while the other turned her left ear to Obianuju's direction expecting answer from the young girl.

"I am coming from the river," Obianuju said innocently.

"Which river?" the other woman asked.

"The river behind the palm tree," Obianuju replied.

"Uzoakoli river, abomination, abomination!! Umunneoma eeh-eh-eeh! ... abomination!!" the women cried out.

Some of the people living nearby ran towards the direction with their matchets and cutlasses and others with their sword.

"What is it woman?" one of the men boldly asked.

"This girl fetched water at Uzoakoli River on an Eke market day ... look at her," she said pointing at Obianuju who was trembling in fear. She is new in Umunneoma and never knew that it was an abomination to fetch water from *Uzoakoli* River on Eke market day. The penalty for such offence is death by stoning. The men around dropped their matchets in dismay and shock. It was resounding in their hearts and they wondered how the poor girl would make such a costly mistake.

"There is nothing we can do. We shall take her to *Ogwugwu,* the Chief Priest" Nwajiuba reluctantly said. The news spread round the village like wildfire and people drew nearer to the scene. Akuebuka, Obianuju's uncle came to the scene in total disappointment.

"Obianuju, what have you done?" he asked in a loud voice. "Why have you done this?

Why couldn't you tell me before leaving?" Many questions were uttered by Akuebuka. He is a respected elder in Umunneoma and one of the most influential, but was quiet aware that his influence cannot make any change. Of course the penalty is death. He is among the council of elders who make laws and he can neither bend nor break it in his favour. Obianuju was ashamed of herself. She had many questions to answer and did not know where to begin, but what she could only say was that she did not know the custom of the people.

She was being dragged to the shrine amidst fierce chanting of the people,

"*Obianuju mere aru,*
O mere aru o.

Gini ka omere?
Ochuru iyi n'ubochi Eke,
Ubochi obodo na aso nso,
Ubochi chi ji echu iyi.

Gini ka nke a putara?
O putara na oburulanu nwa nza,
Nke rijuru afo,
Puta ka ya na chi ya gba mgba."

She was asked to carry the pot of water and was being flogged by the crowd. They were holding their stone at the other hand, only waiting for Ogwugwu to sanction her death by stoning. The voices of the people were heard by Ogwugwu far away. He wondered what must have happened, he kept quiet and began to listen to the song. He then understood the situation of things and shook his head saying, "not again; oh poor dear."

The villagers arrived at the shrine in a little moment. They looked fierce and threatening and ready to abide by the law. Yes, the law by stoning to death.

"*Ogwugwu*, the messenger of the gods, we greet you.

We bring to you this woman, she was caught fetching water at the river on an Eke market day which is against our custom," Ogbubie rightly said.

Ogwugwu looked up to the sky and pointed his hands towards the shining sun and said,

"Let the skies bear us witness,
The sun and every living creature,
as we are about to stone you.
Let your blood never be on our head,
nor on the head of our children."

"Ise hhh …" the crowd responded.
"Take her to the village square and stone her to death, according to our tradition. She must die."

"No, she will not!! She has done nothing wrong!!" The people looked around to see who was saying that. It was a fair creature with white hair and face and a white robe whom people call "the white man." They ran into the scene and claimed to be led by a spirit, they call "Holy."

"Let her go, or stone me instead." The people were afraid to raise their hands on the white man because they have always seen and addressed them as 'Ghosts'. Instead of stoning the white man, they ran away from the scene. The white man and his converts untied Obianuju and took her away. Tears of joy were rolling down the cheeks of Obianuju. She wondered what could have happened to her if the white men didn't come. She was very grateful to the white men and the next morning she was baptized with the Christian name - Mary.

Obianuju then joined Ngozika, her friend as one of the converts of the white men. They were taught about the new God. Obianuju gets shock whenever this new God was attributed as the "Almighty" and "All Powerful."

"What does the white man celebrate every day?" Obianuju asked.

"They celebrate Mass, which is a sacrifice to the Christian God." Ngozika responded. "Oh, they even offer sacrifices."

"Yes with the blood of Jesus Christ."

'Who is this man, you always call his name?"

Ngozika then pointed to a cross with an image on it.

"What is he doing there on the cross?",

"he died for our sins by being crucified."

"Hmmm … if He is all powerful, why then did he allow himself to be crucified?"

"The will of God must always be done."

Obianuju then nodded in hope. She has found a new faith and there are a lot to learn and understand about the mysteries surrounding this God. It was the beginning of a new life for Obianuju, her fate merited her new faith.

Chapter 13

It was a bright morning in Umuabali, the day was growing in a busy scenario. The street was busy with market women carrying their goods to the market to be sold to their desperate customers. Some carried theirs on the head, while others on their rickety bicycles. Little children followed their parents to the market and helped them out in carrying the goods and inviting the customers to buy from them. Most at times, their happy gesture attract customers to buy from them. Children were always said to have good *chi* and the parents keep them in front of the goods to attract success in business. This is a belief in the African-igbo society.

A strange object came into the village with a human being inside it. This object was called 'car' by the white men. Some of the villagers ran away when this object wanted to pass through the market.

"A big fish has run out of our stream." This was the saying of the people. They ran out leaving their goods behind. A pregnant woman nearly lost her baby while running. The market was rowdy and full of confusion.

A young looking man came out of the car; he was Osuoha, son of Mazi Nduka. He left the village to the city for over twenty years and everybody thought he must have been dead. He looked different and now dressed like a white man.

"Come back my people. It's me" Osuoha exclaimed.

People could not believe him because they were still afraid. Ikechi was brave enough to approach him; he placed his hand on the ground, collected a handful of sand and poured on Osuoha. This was to prove that he was human not a spirit. He ran towards him and hugged him. Then the people were able to touch him and the new object - the car.

It was something obvious that everybody in the market wanted to touch the new object. Osuoha's colleagues from Sea Man Oil Company were very much embarrassed at the attitude of the people. They almost tore his clothes when they were welcoming him. The children saw and were amazed as the car moved to his father's compound. On their arrival at the compound, his reception was full of tears; the poor mother never knew that she would one day see her son back on his feet before she would join her ancestors. She danced joyfully and thanked her *chi* for the protection of her son who just became a full fleshed man. *"Oh chi m, nwa m erula ihe eji nwoke eme."* This she sang in a song accompanied with rhythm.

The elders came together to give him 'a red carpet welcome'. They called the people together and Osuoha was entertained with the *Abigbo* cultural dance by the male and female folk. Children in their numbers sang their song, Itempe, exchanging pleasantries with their 'big uncle'. Passers-by in the village wondered who this young man could be that all the villagers participated in the reception. People from the neighboring villages of Nkwoaba, Ezichigbo and Umualumaku drew nearer to celebrate him too.

Ezemmuo was invited to the forum, and as a lover of good things, he quickly hurried to the village square. He began to dance two kilometres away from the scene. Ezemmuo always appreciate people who are successful in life and asks favour from the gods for his own blessing one day.

On his arrival, he was to welcome Osuoha on behalf of the entire community. He cleared his throat twice, looked up to the skies and said 'Our *chi* has done it again. Our sacrifices are beginning to be answered. Our son Osuoha who has left the village for years has just returned. For this reason my people, progress has returned … unity has returned … peace has returned."

The people answered 'Iseeh' at the end of each request. Osuoha was finally given the chance to address his people.

He stood up from his stool and looked into the eyes of his people and said,

"*Ulo Ndi anyi*, I am happy and proud to be a son of the soil. In a special way am also happy to come back to my land. It is exactly twenty years since I left the village for good and I am also back for good."

The people clapped. He laughed and continued.

"I have come to bring development into the land of Umuabali with my colleagues. The gods have blessed our land with oil which we have come to utilize for our good. Our youths shall be employed to help out in the work. Before the end of this year and this land will truly become our home", he said.

The people were very much happy and the music continued to play.

The following day, the youths of Umuabali came out en mass at the village square with their hearts to begin the work earnestly. The workers of the Sea Mans Oil Company came out also to take them on a one-day orientation programme. Mr Fred, the secretary general, was to take them on the orientation. He was strict and the youths did not feel comfortable with him, especially whenever he uses deteriorating words to qualify them as "animals and black monkeys." Mr Fred said that Africans do not have 'soul', and this triggered a serious quarrel between him and the youths. They broke his head and he began to bleed. He withdrew every support he gave to them and promised them serious attacks. The youth sent him out of the village and asked him to go to hell with his worthless offer.

Osuoha was not happy with this incident when it happened. His colleagues refused to do any job with him in that land any longer because of the assault the secretary general received.

Osuoha then invited another colleague from Home Base Oil Company. They came and complained that the people were more ignorant than beasts. Osuoha swallowed the assault and told them not to say that before the people that they may not get upset. They began the drilling of the oil the following day and were exporting to foreign countries, while counting their profits in millions.

Osuoha selfishly abandoned the projects and for over six months, nothing was done for the village, not even a single stone was laid down. The people began to smell foul play. The first step they took was to call Osuoha to order and reminded him of his promises. He promised them again that the work would begin in four market days. The people waited patiently until the four market days were over. On the eight market day, the villagers went to him for their compensation. He ran away from the village with his colleagues. It was a big disappointment to the entire community and his immediate family.

"He has milked our land and ran away with our money." This was the saying of every person. Meanwhile, the farmlands were ravaged. Their cassava farm and even their vegetables were turned to swamp. They felt another sorrow once again from Osuoha and his white men friends. They had sworn to deal with any white man that would come into their land. Thus, Osuoha their pride became their failure.

Chapter 14

A certain group of white men sailed into Umuabali
Kingdom. This time, with some Africans as their followers.
These white men were dressed in white robes and didn't
seem to have toes. The ugly incident between Umuabali
people and Osuoha's white men colleagues drew them
almost crazy. The result was that they were ready to deal
with the white men if any should touch their soil.

Obianuju led the white men across the streams from
Umunneoma, her mother's people, to Umuabali, her
hometown, to spread the Gospel of the new God. Mazi
Okosis became disappointed with his daughter when
he saw her following the ways of the white men. She
asked her father to help the white men with one hut where
they would spend the night after each day. Mazi Okosis
reluctantly gave them a hut to live but he warned her
daughter of the implication of what she was doing but
she said,

"The God I worship is supreme,
nothing will happen to me.
These men saved my life and also saved my soul,
I owe them a lot, father."

They remembered how the white men saved the life of their daughter, Nneoma, Obianuju's mother, went to the white men and welcomed them to their land.

The people summoned Obianuju at the village square and flogged her mercilessly for harboring the white men in their house. Meanwhile, the white men were already doing good things in the life of some people they had encountered and the story about the white men changed amongst some of the members of the community.

The youths organized a troop to Obianuju's house to force the white men out of the village. On their arrival, they were marvelled how Ikemba who has been ill for over six market days was miraculously cured by the white man's drug.

Instead of harming the white men, their attitude changed into witnessing the recovery of the young man. The white men spoke to them through their interpreter.

"Tell them that I welcome them to my hut", Nwadishi would interpret it in a way the people would hear.

"Whiteman is saying welcome." The youths nodded in acceptance.

"Please ask them why they are holding matchets and sticks, Who are they going to attack?"

"The white man is asking you why you are carrying all these.", Nwadishi said.

Uzo spoke on behalf of the youths, "We have come to ask you what you want from us." The youths nodded in agreement because Uzo spoke what was in their mind.

"They said they came to know what you have come for."

"Tell them that I have come for peace."

"The white man said that he came for our peace", Nwadishi happily said.

"What peace, we have heard that so many times" Chikadibia angrily said.

"Tell them that I have come to bring peace, the good news and love of our Lord Jesus Christ, the saviour of the world."

"The white man said he has come to bring peace and tell you about his new God, Jesus Christ."

"New God? what does that mean?" Uzo asked.

"They said they want to know" Nwadishi told the white man.

"My God is supreme over all your gods. He created you and wants you to be his followers."

The white man said that his God is powerful than your gods, that his new God created us and his new God wants us to be his follower.

"Taa! Abomination!" the youths exclaimed.

"Tell him to stop speaking ill of the gods or else Amadioha will strike him dead. I am not going to take part in this discussion" Uzo said and left the compound and the other youths followed him.

Eze and Obika were the only people that waited and asked the white men to teach them about their new God. The white men told them about their new God and they believed. The white men were delighted in their belief. They baptized them with the name 'James and John' respectively. They joined the group of converts and now followed the white men around the village.

The white men gave them gifts and they thanked them. Obika's mothers cried loudly when she heard that her son ate the white man's gift, because it was believed that whoever eats anything belonging to the white men has been contaminated. News spread like wide fire that Eze and Obika have finally accepted the white man's ways and even ate the white man's gift. It became an interesting topic for market women and girls coming back from the stream.

One Afor market day, two maidens were coming back from the stream, they were gossiping about the white men and their new converts when suddenly they saw the white men trying to pass through their route. They screamed and broke their pots full of water and ran away.

"Why are they scared of us?" the white men asked some of the converts. "They see you as people whom their gods have cursed and any contact made with them might contaminate them'.

"Really, people and ignorance", the white man laughed.

The elders of Umuabali gathered to find solution to the white man's issue. Ezemmuo was present at the deliberation. The fact was that the white men seem to be of help to the people and some of the people now worship the white man's God to the detriment of the gods of the land.

Ezemmuo was very much disappointed at the elder who talked in favour of the white men.

"Perhaps, the white men have used their medicine to breastfeed them to accept his ways', he said.

Ezemmuo did not want to take any decision on what to do to the white men because of the love the people were already developing with them. He instead held his peace and swallowed his words.

Chapter 15

It was an Eke market day, Ezemmuo called the people together at the village square to address them on the most pertinent issue. He told them that tomorrow would be exactly the end of the market weeks given to them by the gods to find the *ofo*.

> "My people, it is with deep sorrow that I have come to announce to you that the warriors are not yet back from their long trip and tomorrow will be exactly the end of the market weeks the gods have given."

The people began to feel sorrowful and began to mourn. They were to remain at the village square to see if any of them would come back.

Some of the youths were sent to mount at different routes to notify the people whenever any of the warriors would be back. The villagers were in the square waiting all through the day, and there did not seem to be any sign of any warrior coming back. Some fell asleep. Ezemmuo and the elders were in fear thinking of what must have happened to them. It was a day of sorrow.

One of the youths ran suddenly from the eastern direction to the village square. He ran like one who had fought with a lion.

"He is back … he is back!!" the youth said. The women sleeping woke up and everybody began to ask,

"Who is back?"

"I saw him" he spoke quickly.

"Obidozie … Obidozie. He is back"

"Ehh …" the people exclaimed.

They stood up and everyone kept looking at the direction of the East to see him. After some minutes, they saw a staggering man coming. They looked at him with keen interest. It was Obidozie the warrior, in his right hand was the *ofo* which he left to search with his co-warriors.

"Where are the other warriors?" Ezemmuo asked.

"They are all dead", he said breathing heavily.

"The last of them were Nnaemeka and Oguzie, the three of us brought the *ofo* but on our way back we were attacked by forest beasts. The beasts ate them up but I escaped," He said.

"Ehh …" the people exclaimed and tears began to fall from their cheeks. Ezemmuo looked up to the skies and shaded tears too, but as a man he held his sorrow, cleared his throat and said, "My people cry no more, the gods have answered our prayers. Our son, the warrior is back, let not your tears deny you of happiness." He carried the *ofo* from Obidozie and showed to the people, "our son has brought back the *ofo*."

They shouted in happiness and welcomed Obidozie with joy and cheers from all. The day was becoming darker and the people spent the moon light play at the village square that night.

Obianuju was delighted when she heard that Obidozie was back. She was happy to have him back. She hugged him and thanked God for the protection given to Obidozie. She told him everything that happened while he was away, especially, how she was nearly killed by her mother's people, and about her new faith. Obidozie was very angry in the first place, but with time he began to believe what Obianuju was telling him about the Christian God.

Obianuju introduced Obidozie to the white missionaries and they were surprise when they heard that the people believe that the Igwe's soul will not be at rest until *Ofo* was placed on his body.

The white missionaries taught Obidozie about their new God and to Obianuju's greatest surprise, Obidozie believed at last. The elders called Obidozie and told him that he would he coronated by sunrise and he has to select a wife from the maidens as his suitor before he could be coroneted.

Obidozie told them that he would marry Obianuju. The elders disagreed because Obianuju is from an Osu family, and it is believed that they are dedicated to the gods as servants to the gods.

"No ... she is no longer a servant to the gods but a servant of the living God."

The elders had no option than to allow him make his choice.

"Gom ... gom ... gom" was the sound of the ogene, the drum that awakes the sun. It was the happiest day in the kingdom of Umuabali. The children ran round the village with shouts of joy. The people all gathered at the usual village square, including those from the other villages.

"We have come to place the Ofo on the body of our late Igwe whom our enemies killed. We are also going to crown a new Igwe whom the gods have chosen," the people clapped.

"Obidozie and Obianuju," Ezemmuo called.

"Yes, Ezemmuo" they answered.

"Come forward and knee before the people." Obidozie came and knelt before the people. Ezemmuo cleared his throat twice and said:

> "I call upon the gods as I place this *Ofo* on
> the body of our late Igwe. May the gods
> accept his soul. May he find peace with
> our ancestors. May he always direct us."

The people responded "Iseeh" at the end of each request.

He turned to Obidozie and said "my son, with the power bestowed on me as, the messenger of the gods and Onowu of this kingdom. I hereby crown you Igwe. Following your strength, courage and bravery to save our people I give you the title of *Ochiedike* 1 of Umuabali kingdom."

"Igwe" the people shouted and exchanged greetings with Obidozie and his wife Obianuju who are now wearing the crown as Igwe and Lolo.

Ezemmuo now asked Obidozie to address his people the first time as the Igwe;

'My people, I thank you all for the honour you have given me and for finding me worthy to be your Igwe. I salute the memory of my fellow warriors who laid down their lives in defence of our father land. We shall not forget them. May their souls rest in peace. As your Igwe, I am only the servant and you are the masters.

I promise to serve you well."

He cleared his throat and said "This is a new beginning in our land, therefore from now, our kingdom shall no longer be answering *Umuabali*, we shall now be answering *Umuihe*, meaning 'children of light'. Also, we are no longer going to worship our gods, we have now renounced them. We shall worship the Almighty God who created heaven and earth"

He said and called the white missionaries. The missionaries came and taught the people about their God. Igwe asked Ezemmuo to bring the carved woods and image of the gods and they were burnt to ashes. Obidozie was baptized with the Christian name Peter, because he was to be the leader of the people and Ezemmuo was baptised with the Christian name, Paul. The entire people of Umuabali were baptised and they now worship the white man's God.

While the celebration was still in progress, Osuoha came back to the village. The youths ran to attack him but Igwe Obidozie asked them not to harm him. Osuoha bent down on his knees and begged his people to forgive him all that he did to them and promised to fulfill all that he promised them. Obidozie assured him that he has been forgiven.

He brought back the money he ran away with and commenced development. He first built a Church where the people worshipped the new God, after which he commenced the building of a health centre for the sick and maternity home for the pregnant women. Construction of roads, pipe borne water followed immediately. Things really changed. Obianuju gave birth to a baby boy, who was to be the heir to the throne, and he was named "*Onochie*," he was baptized with the Christian name "Solomon." Obianuju's parents were really proud of her. This was the beginning of sunrise in the land and the people continued to beat the drums of sunrise.

ACKNOWLEGEMENTS

'Gratitude' they say is a less virtue, but ingratitude is the highest vice. It is on this note that I wish to thank the Almighty God for making this debut a reality.

I thank my beloved Parents, Mr. and Mrs. Joseph Igbokwe for their parental care and supports. I thank my brothers; Simon, Charles, Donald and Cajethan Igbokwe for understanding my long night in the computer. I thank my big sister Jane Anugwara and her husband Ken for being there for me always.

Thank you dear uncle, Rev. and Mrs. Francis Ben Amaechi and family for your fervent prayers.

I thank my Archbishop, Most Rev. Anthony J.V. Obinna, The Priests, Religious and Laity of Owerri Archdiocese and their efforts towards eradication of Osu caste system in Igboland.

I thank in a special way, the Formators and Seminarians of Assumpta Minor Seminary, Naze and St. Peter Claver Seminary, Okpala and the Members of the Elites Press Club of Nigeria for their supports.

The *Mikadoz,* my friends and Colleagues, I thank you all for being very supportive, your names are innumerable to mention.

I am very grateful to Chimamanda Ngozi Adichie for teaching me my right to tell my own story and Esq. Reginald Akagha for teaching me how dangerous words can be in a careless mouth.

May I use this opportunity to thank my friends who are part of my success story, Maribeth Giese Stevens, Peter Littlefield, Kenneth Posner, Eddie Kenny and not forgetting Peter Lawrence, Shirlem Kim, Jessa Paxton and Michelle Chandler.

In a more special way, I thank Rev. Fr. Paschal Chiekezi, Rev. Sr. Mary Joy Emeribe, Chief (Mrs.) Theresa Okonkwo and Dr. (Mrs) Nma Olebara for Proof-reading my work, making useful suggestions and writing the foreword to my book.

Thanks you all for being there for me when I needed you most.

Jisie nu Ike.

ABOUT THE BOOK

This book is a product of articulate and reflective exploration of facts about a typical pre-christian Igbo community, Umuabali, characterized by some heinous practices such as the worship of many deities and the Osu Caste System. Through the advent of Christianity, there was a transition from Umuabali (Children of darkness) to Umuihe (Children of Light). I praise the reflective and imaginative prowess of the author in this epic. I therefore recommend this masterpiece to all who wish to understand how Christianity can bring light to our darkened world by beating the 'Drums of sunrise.'

-Rev. Fr. Paschal Chiekezi.

Sixtus Chetachi Igbokwe has in this novel 'Drums of Sunrise' disclosed his intellectual identity, personality, capacity, potentiality and prowess in creative writing.

The novel teaches love, hardwork, dedication, perseverance, humility, patience and discourages pride, egotism, vainglory and deceit. I recommend that this book be made compulsory for all students. I also recommend it to the public. It is a must read for every home. I congratulate Sixtus Chetachi Igbokwe for the job well done.

-Dr. (Mrs.) Nma Olebara (FCAI).

Drums of Sunrise is a captivating story set in South-Eastern Nigeria during the pre-colonial era of the 1890's. Sixtus Chetachi Igbokwe has in his debut presented us with an insight into the African-Igbo society, a people who draw their life from their culture and who later embraced Christianity by the coming of the white men. This moment became a turning point in their life. I praise the Author's creativity and therefore recommend this book to the general public.

-Chief (Mrs.) Theresa Okonkwo.

ABOUT THE AUTHOR

Sixtus Chetachi Igbokwe was born in South Eastern Nigeria in 1996. He is a native of Umuonyeali Mbieri in Mbaitolu L.G.A of Imo State, Nigeria. He is an alumnus of Assumpta Minor Seminary, Naze and St. Peter Claver Seminary, Okpala Imo State, Nigeria. He is a member Association of Nigerian Authors (ANA). He enjoys reading, writing, and teaching. *Drums of Sunrise* is his debut.

Printed in the United States
By Bookmasters